This Little Tiger book belongs to:

_____

_____

_____

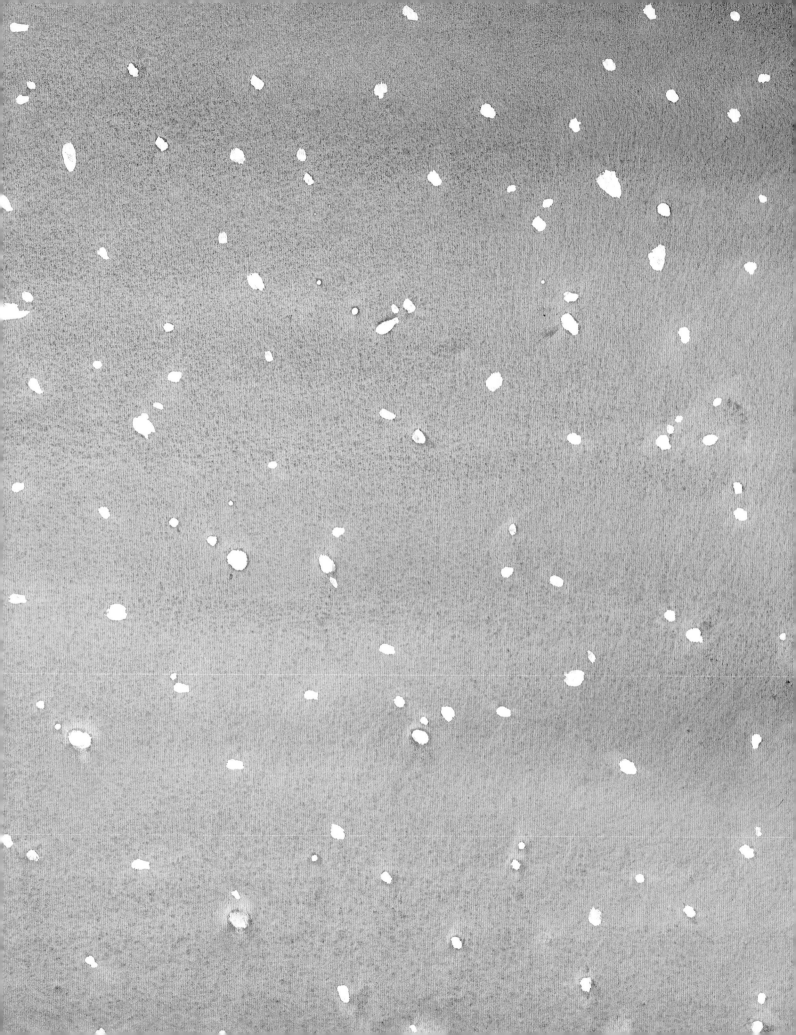

For my Mother —
who doesn't like staying in bed either!
~ M. C.

For Tony Downham
~ G. W.

LITTLE TIGER PRESS
1 The Coda Centre, 189 Munster Road, London SW6 6AW
www.littletiger.co.uk
First published in Great Britain 1996
by Little Tiger Press, London
This edition published 2013
Text copyright © Michael Coleman 1996
Illustrations copyright © Gwyneth Williamson 1996
Michael Coleman and Gwyneth Williamson have
asserted their rights to be identified as the author
and illustrator of this work under the Copyright,
Designs and Patents Act, 1988
All rights reserved • ISBN 978-1-84895-783-1
Printed in China • LTP/1900/0685/0613
2 4 6 8 10 9 7 5 3 1

Ridiculous!

Michael Coleman

Gwyneth Williamson

LITTLE TIGER PRESS

"Ho hum," yawned Mr. Tortoise. "Winter is here."
"So it is," yawned Mrs. Tortoise. "Come on,
Shelley, time for bed."

"But I don't feel sleepy yet," said Shelley.

"Ridiculous!" cried Mr. Tortoise. "All tortoises
go to sleep for the winter."

"Why?" asked Shelley.

"Because it's cold outside, and there's no food."

"But I don't want to go to sleep," said Shelley.
"I want to see what winter is like!"

"*Ridiculous!*" cried Mr. and Mrs. Tortoise together.
"Whoever heard of a tortoise outside in winter?"

Soon
Mr. Tortoise
began to snore...

and not long after
that, Mrs. Tortoise
began to snore...

and not long after *that*, Shelley left her warm bed of leaves, and out she went through a hole in the shed to see what winter was like.

Outside the shed, Shelley blinked. There was snow and ice everywhere, even on the duck pond and the hill. As she lumbered along, a duck spotted her.

"A tortoise out in winter?" quacked the duck. "*Ridiculous!*"

"No it isn't," said Shelley.

"Oh, no? Then let's see you break through the ice to get food like *I* can. Ha-quack-ha!"

"He's right," thought Shelley. "I can't do that. I don't have a beak."

As Shelley began to walk up the hill, she met
a dog.

"A tortoise out in winter?" barked the dog.
"*Ridiculous!*"

"No it isn't," said Shelley, feeling a little cross.
"Oh, no? Then let's see you keep warm by running around like *I* can. Ha-woof-ha!"
"He's right," thought Shelley sadly. "I can't do that, either."

The dog ran off after a cat, but the cat climbed up a tree. She looked down at Shelley.

"A tortoise out in winter?" meowed the cat. *"Ridiculous!"*

"No it isn't," said Shelley, even more crossly.

"Oh, no? Then let's see you run into a nice warm house as quickly as *I* can. Ha-meow-ha!"

"She's right," thought Shelley, shivering with cold. "I can't run like a dog or a cat. I'm just too slow!"

The cat raced off into her house before the dog could catch her, and Shelley trudged toward the top of the hill, where she met a bird.

"A tortoise out in winter?" cheeped the bird.
"*Ridiculous!*"

"No it isn't," snapped Shelley.

"Oh no? Then let's see you fly home
and cuddle up with your family like *I* can.
Ha-cheep-ha!"

"Of course I can't fly," thought Shelley.
"I can't even hop!"

Shelley felt cold and miserable. She remembered her
warm, cozy bed, and a tear trickled down her cheek.
"They're *all* right," she thought. "A tortoise out in
winter *is* ridiculous!"

She was so sad she didn't notice the big patch of
ice ahead . . .

and she slipped on it!
  Shelley fell over backward
and began to slide down the hill.
Faster and faster she went...

...faster than
a *dog* could run...

faster than
a *cat*...

until suddenly she
hit a bump . . .

and flew into the air
like a *bird*.

With a thump Shelley landed on the icy duck pond and slid toward the hole in the shed, but it was all covered up with ice!

"Ha-quack-ha, what did I say?"
cried the duck as she slid by him.
"Where's your beak to break through the ice?"
"I don't have a beak," thought Shelley.
"But I *do* have . . ."

"*...a shell!*"
And tucking her head inside it,
she broke through the ice,
into the shed and home!

Hearing all the noise, Mrs. Tortoise woke up.
"You haven't been outside, have you, Shelley?"
she asked.

"A tortoise out in winter?" said Shelley,
snuggling into bed. And before she could say
"Ridiculous!"
she was fast asleep.

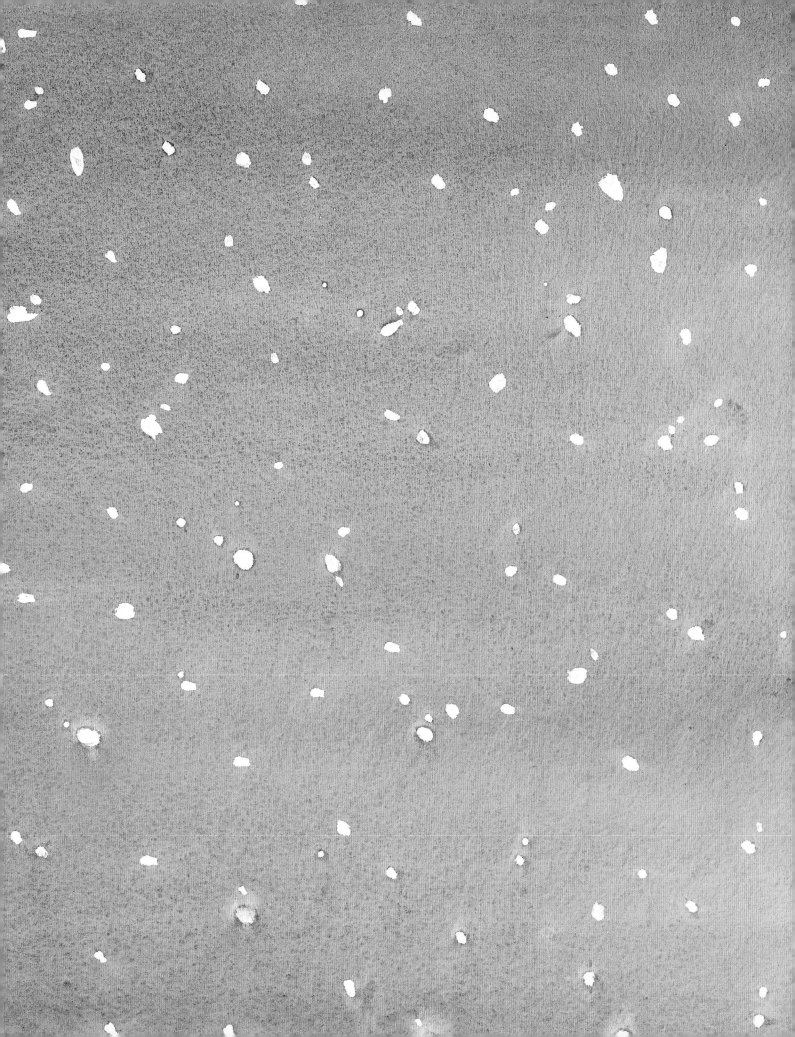